AF437935
Who is Dapkamio's friend ?

Come and join us on
our adventure !

GRAPHICS

NUMBERS

REWARD

PREFACE

Let them eat the biggest piece of cake...

Let the window seat be theirs...

Let them always smile; let them remain far away from the

winds of fears.

Our wishes for our children don't stop there. Whilst we wish to give

them the world, we are shaping their worlds at the same time in

incredibly important ways.

This is why this starting point is very important...

This 'timeless' book you are now holding, was designed with methods

that bring about successful results regarding the foundations

of their development.

This 'Writing Book' developed in line with scientific research, allows

your children to learn letters and numbers in a joyous manner as they

embark on their intellectual journey.

As it contributes to the skills in 4–6 year olds which are developed

before school, this book also allows the unseen bonds to strengthen

between parent and child.

The pages of this book are filled with methods that allow your children

to develop motor, perception, imagination, bonding, association,

concentration and focus skills as well as habits such as hand–crafting.

S : MOVING THINGS AROUND

C : BRINGING THEM TOGETHER

A : ADAPTATION

M : CHANGING THEM, OR MAKING THEM BIGGER OR SMALLER

P : PLACING THEM IN DIFFERENT POSITIONS

E : GETTING RID OF THINGS OR

R : TURNING AROUND OR REDOING THEM.

SCAMPER METHOD

Your child's mind is an endless universe...

There is an incredible way to reach out to their imagination.

The scamper technique!

This famous method, based on developing creative thinking skills in your children, allows information to come together like puzzle pieces and become embedded in the right place in their minds.

This book you are holding was shaped with brainstorming, learning philosophy, association techniques and teachings based on the Scamper method.

COME ON, TOGETHER LETS:

- Discover your children's skills
- Develop their different thinking capabilities
- Engrain written culture in our children
- Help them gain self confidence
- Give them the opportunity to use their senses
- And give the possibility to create something new

ARE WE READY?

If your answer is 'Yes', then please turn the pages of this book... The colourful road to reach your children's mind is awaiting you!

AUTHOR
Axel Kamalak

Thanks

Many thanks for your precious help.

PSYCHOLOGIST
Virginie Bouchon

SPEECH PATHOLOGISTS
Camille Molinier

PSYCHO-MOTOR THERAPIST
Agathe Roussel

DAPKAM
édition

With their funny makeup, colourful hair and funny facial expressions, clowns put on comedy shows. These shows are sometimes put on stage, sometimes they are in films. Dapkamio thought… If he was a clown, what would he wear? A yellow bow-tie. Red and fluffy hair. And a polka-dot costume! He/she would have so much fun and also surprise his friends who wouldn't recognize him. :)

Can you help draw and colour the clown shapes?

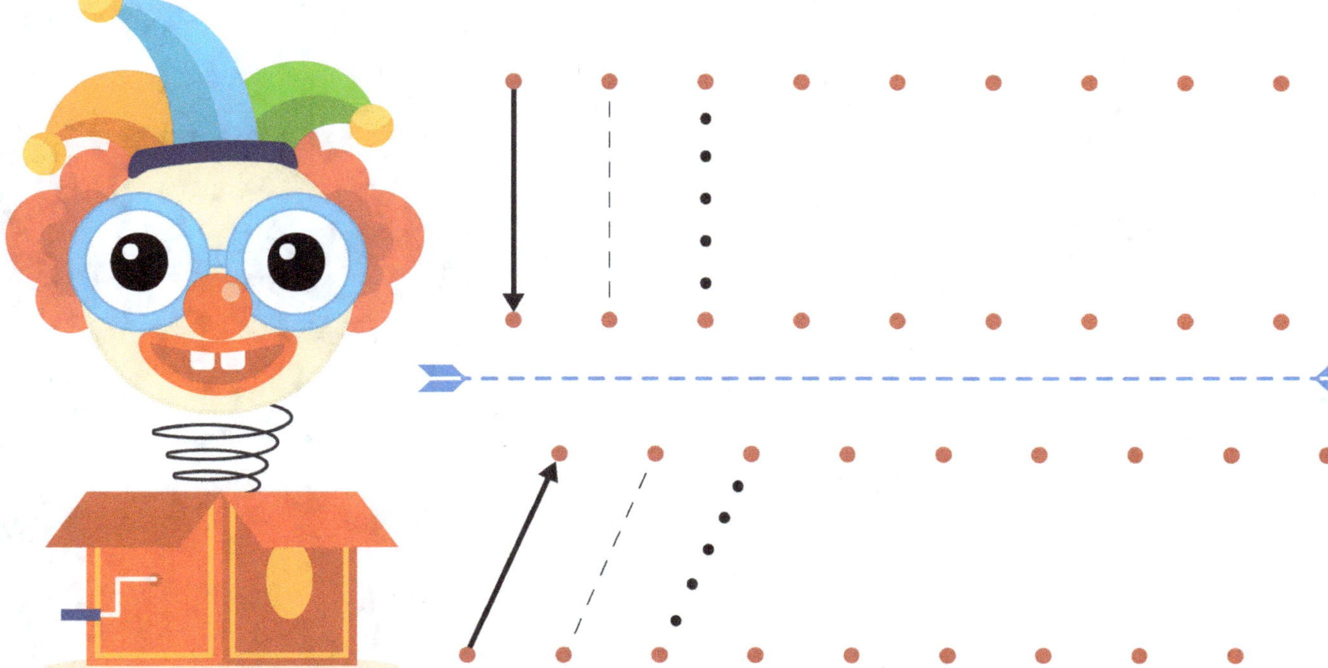

REFLEXION

What colour can a clown's hair be?

IMAGINATION

If you were a clown, how would you like to dress? Can you please draw here?

With your scissors, you can cut out and color the medal at the end of the book.

Your birthday is the name given to the day you were born. It was Dapkamio's birthday, and the cake was going to be cut. He looked at the colourful presents his friends bought with excitement. He lent over to the candles on the cake and made a wish: "I would like the people I love to be happy and would like to get good notes from my classes :)"

What about helping Dapkamio out to help him reach his presents?

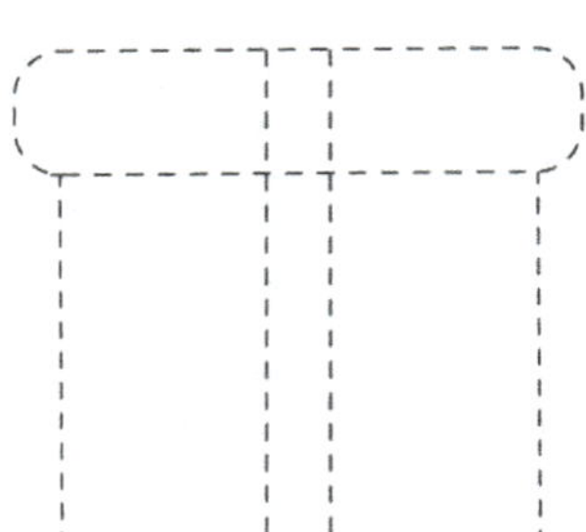

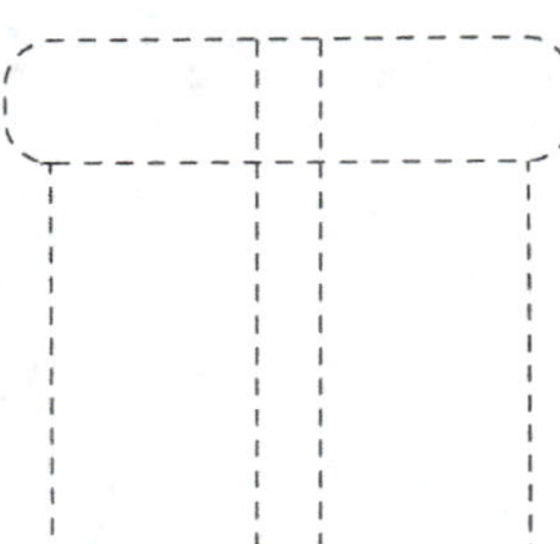

REFLEXION

What happens on birthdays?

IMAGINATION

What kind of presents might have Dapkamio's friends brought him/her?

Can you draw them here please?

Massalto asked… How does a computer connect to the internet? "With the help of a device called a modem" replied her mother. Modems allow communication to take place between networks. And an internet connection is formed due to the relationship between a computer and a modem. Massalto was surprised when she found out that old modems used to be with cables. "What do you mean? Things we write used to travel through the cables?" she said and laughed.

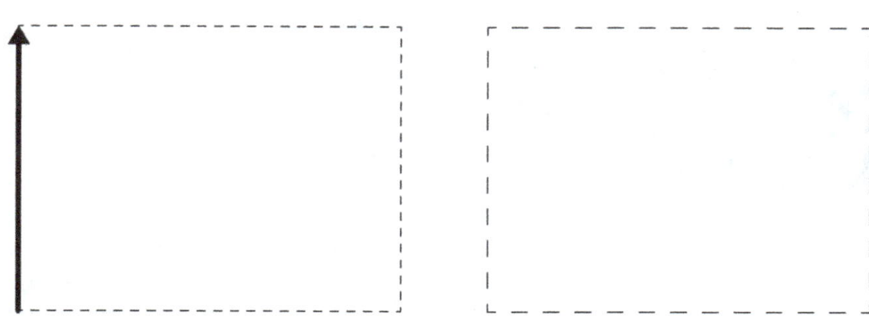

REFLEXION

How is a computer connected to the internet?

IMAGINATION

Could you please draw the cartoon you want to watch on the internet here?

3

Holiday

All children love holidays. Just like Dapkamio! Discovering new places and doing new activities quickens the brain. Dapkamio was so excited and impatient to go on holiday. He thought "what would I like to take with me if I went to a deserted island?" He started packing his suitcases and thought "my pencils should be with me, that way, I can draw everywhere."

Are you ready to draw a holiday suitcase that has wonderful items inside?

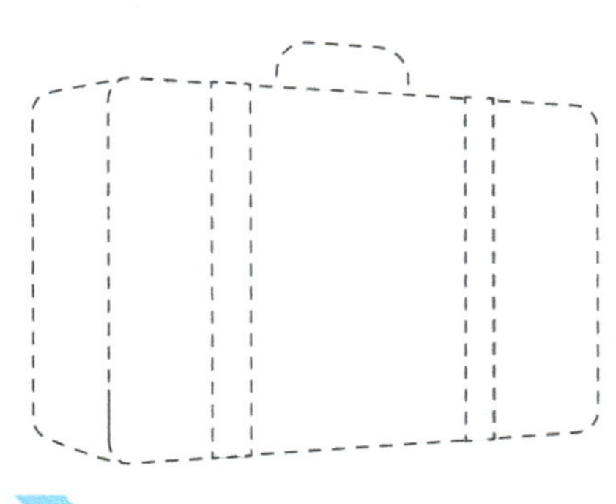

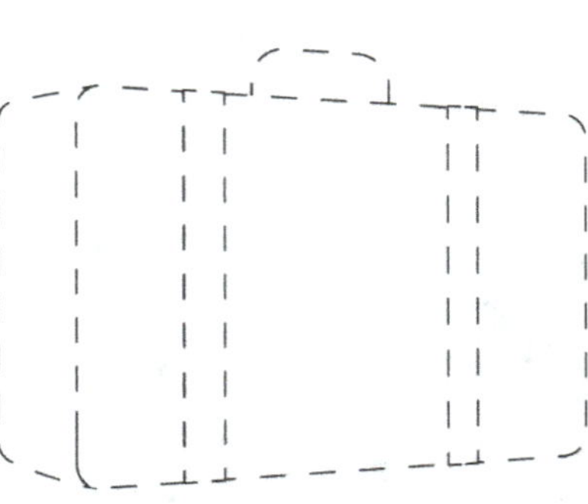

REFLEXION

Why do we go on holiday?

IMAGINATION

You are by the seaside and there is a huge umbrella; how would you use it?

Can you draw it here?

4

✂ With your scissors, you can cut out and color the medal at the end of the book.

The Christmas Tree was filled with decorations. Dapkamio wondered about the gifts under the tree whilst watching the mesmerizing lights that decorated the tree. What were in the gifts?

A remote-controlled car would be great. Or a toy robot... Maybe a musical instrument...

"Some trees give oxygen to us, some give gifts", said Dapkamio.

Are you ready to draw on top of the squares using a pencil in the best way possible?

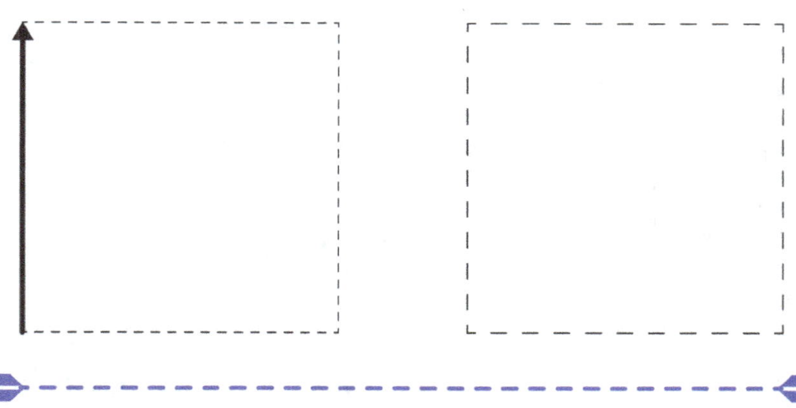

REFLEXION

What was Dapkamio wondering?

IMAGINATION

What could be inside the gifts under the Christmas tree? Could you draw them here?

5

Animal Friends

Dapkamio threw the small ball in his hand further away… His dog friend ran up to it quickly, picked it up in his mouth and brought it back to Dapkamio. They were playing together and having fun together. Massalto, who saw this said "I should have a dog." She thought, "Good friends never leave each other alone." :)

Are you ready to draw and colour in the small paws and the cute doghouse?

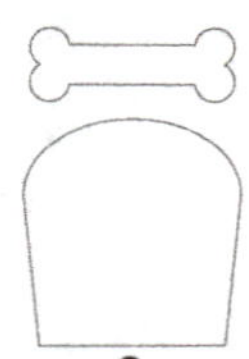 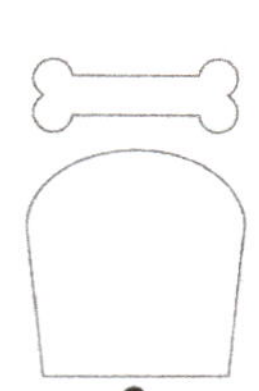 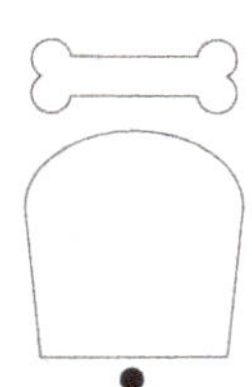 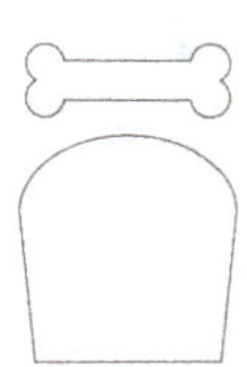

REFLEXION

Why did Massalto want a dog?

IMAGINATION

If you had a dog friend, how would you play with them? Can you draw it here?

6

The Eiffel Tower is the most important symbol of Paris... Every year, hundreds of people from across the globe come to see this iron tower. Massalio imagined going up the Eiffel Tower. "I'd love to see the landscape like birds. But I must go down the stairs since I don't have wings" she said and laughed at the same time.

Are you ready to draw great squares together?

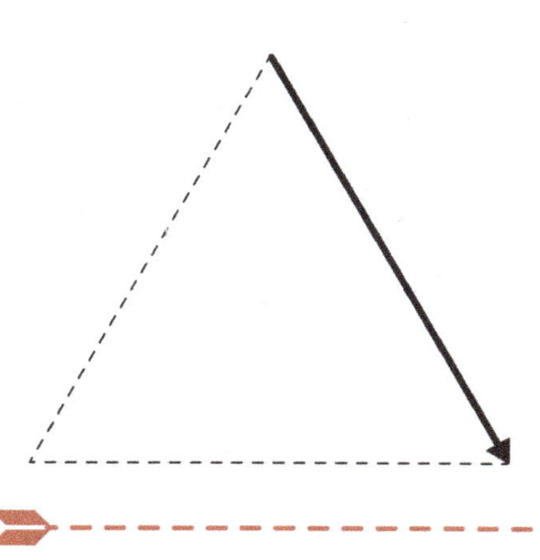

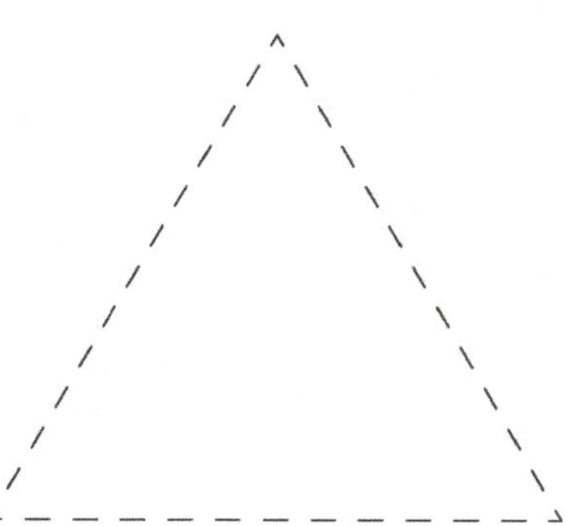

REFLEXION

Where is the Eiffel Tower?

IMAGINATION

What kind of scenery can Massalio see when she goes up onto the Eiffel Tower? Could you draw it here?

7

With your scissors, you can cut out and color the medal at the end of the book.

Kite

Dapkamio was watching the colourful kites in the sky… He had come to a picnic with his family. His dad had told him that flying a kite increases concentration. Dapkamio took his kite and started running against the wind. As he ran, his kite was getting higher. This incredible display was bewitching Dapkamio. :)

Are you ready to draw and colour the pentagon with your pencil?

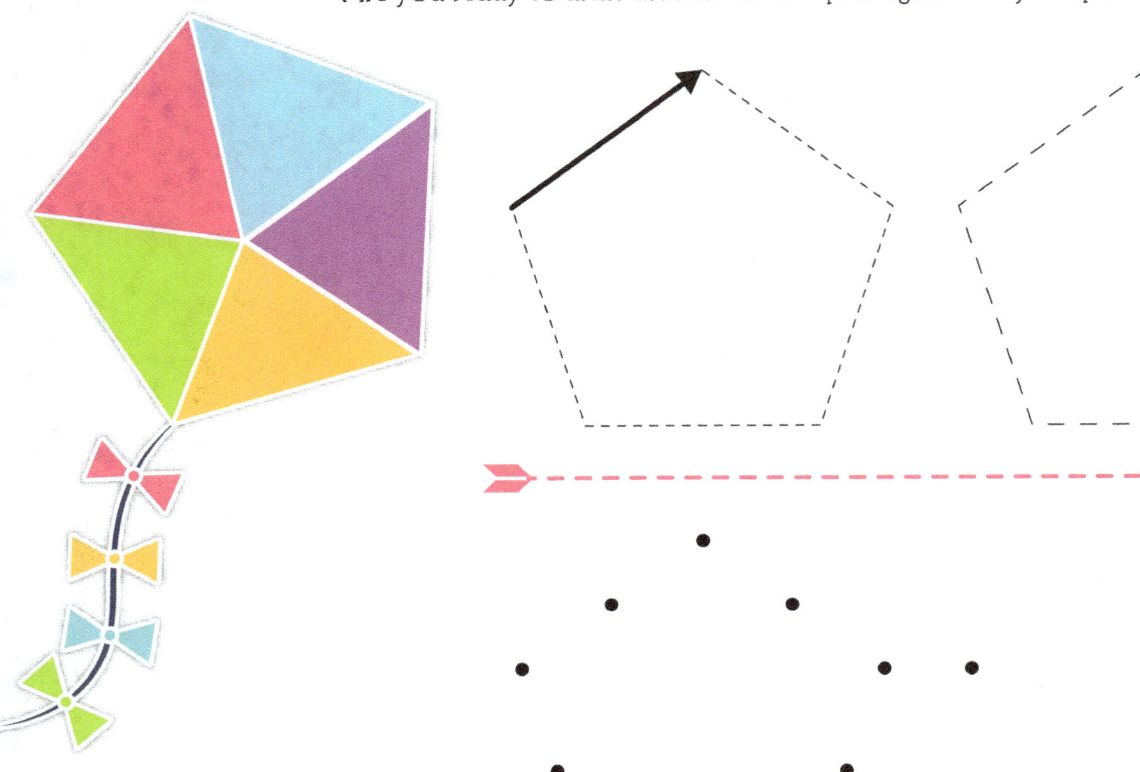

REFLEXION

How are kites flown?

IMAGINATION

What else can we kites for? Can you draw it here?

8

Trapezium

Massalio was in geometry class… She had learned that a trapezium was a shape with four sides. She thought. What could she find around here that looked like a trapezium? A cake tin looked like a trapezium. A vase also looked like a trapezium. Massalio loved learning about new shapes in geometry and using her imagination to draw them. :)

Shall we start drawing trapeziums meticulously?

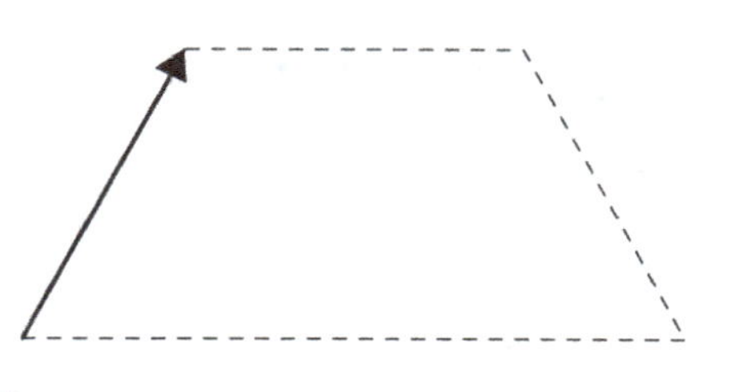

REFLEXION

How many sides does a trapezium have?

IMAGINATION

What is the first thing that comes to mind when you think of the shape of a trapezium?

Bee Hive

Bees are very hardworking. They collect pollen from colourful flowers. They construct their hives in the shape of hexagons. In this way, they can create the most closely packed packets. Isn't this great? Massalto was feeling impatient to share this wonderful information she read in a nature book.

What about drawing and colouring the honeycombs?

REFLEXION

What shape are the hives of bees?

IMAGINATION

How do you think bees collect honey from flowers? Could you draw it?

10

Apple Tree

The apple tree, originating from Central Asia, loves plenty of light and sunshine. It blooms pink and white flowers in spring. Dapkamio's mother placed an apple in his lunchbox and said "An apple will keep you full"... Dapkamio thought for a second. What if watermelons grew on trees? Most probably, the branches wouldn't be able to carry the watermelon's, and they would fall like leaves.

Are you ready to draw an apple tree whilst thinking of a juicy apple?

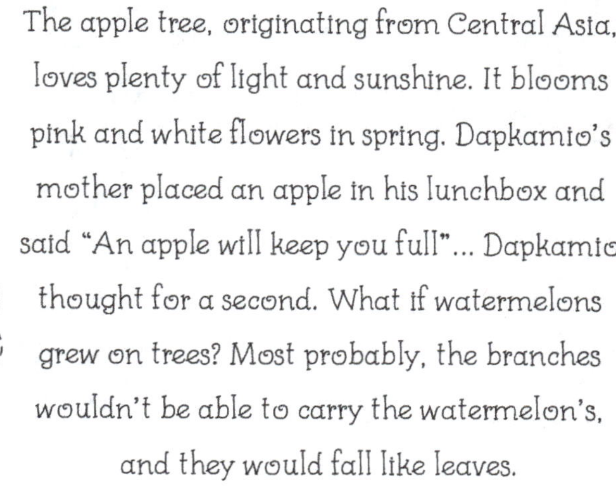

REFLEXION

What colour flowers does the apple tree bloom?

IMAGINATION

What would a completely pink apple tree look like? Can you imagine it and then draw it here?

✂ With your scissors, you can cut out and color the medal at the end of the book.

Balls

It's important to exercise in the open air. Exercise supports growth and development in a healthy way. As muscles are used, bones strengthen. Dapkamio loves to play ball. He thought "How would we play if balls didn't exist?" He remembered the day that he filled his mother's fabrics into a pillow case and played with it like a ball.

Can you colour the beautiful balls carefully?

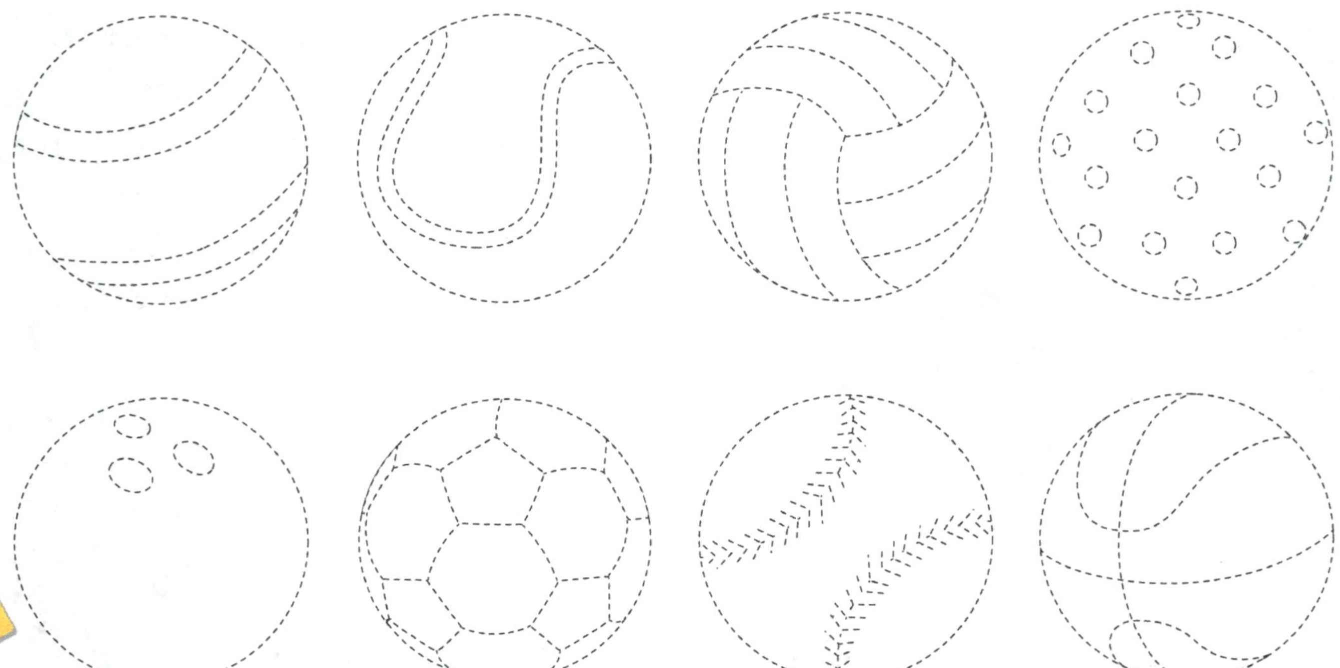

REFLEXION

Why should we exercise?

IMAGINATION

If the balls were really big and heavy, how would the children play games? Can you draw it here?

12

Planet

When you look at our planet earth from space, the world looks like a giant blue globe… It is the unique combination of air, water and soil. Massalio asked "How do children who speak different languages play together?" Then she smiled and said "Hide-and-seek is universal, you don't need to speak the same language to hide or to tag someone."

Are you excited to draw circles that evoke our planet?

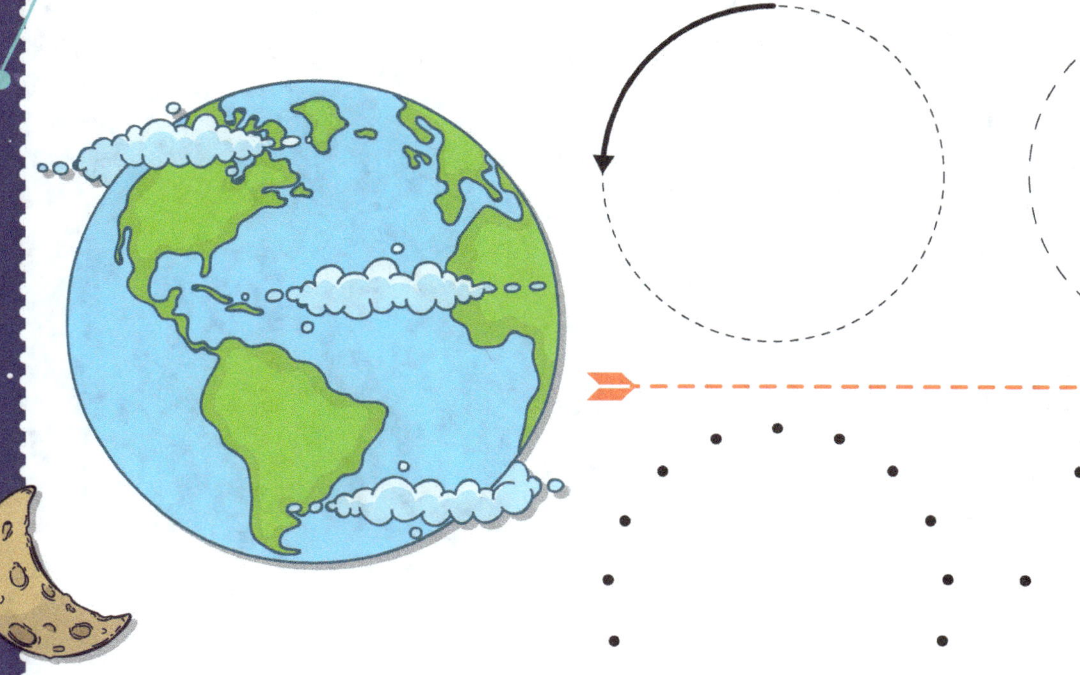

REFLEXION

What does the earth look like when you look at it from space?

IMAGINATION

If you had the highest telescope in the world, what would you like to see? Could you draw it here?

Chicken Eggs

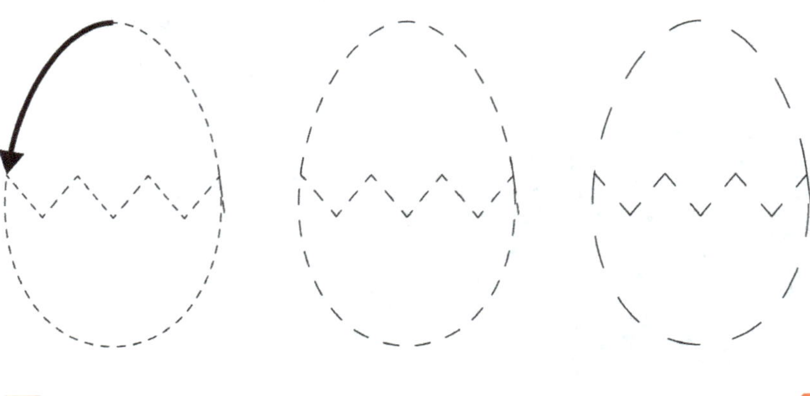

REFLEXION

How are chicks born?

IMAGINATION

Whilst walking on the road, you found a chicken feather. What kind of a feather is it?
Can you draw it here?

14

"Snails are so slow" thought Massalio... "They're moving just like me when I've just woken up in the morning". Snails usually appear when it's just rained. In the winter they gather energy under the soil or in tree pockets. "I would love to be able to teach them how to run, " said Massalio. :)
Are you ready to draw and colour the home that the snail is carrying on its back?

REFLEXION

Where do snails live in winter?

IMAGINATION

If you were to draw a playground for a snail what would you put in it? Could you draw it here?

15

Massalto picked up the sweet jar from the table where her mother had left it and started to eat them one by one. These sweets are so cute… They're multicolored… So, how are these sweets harmful when they taste so good? Massalto's stomach started hurting. The sugar jar had completely emptied. She then realised she had gone a little overboard. :)

Shall we draw and color new sweets to go into the sweet jar?

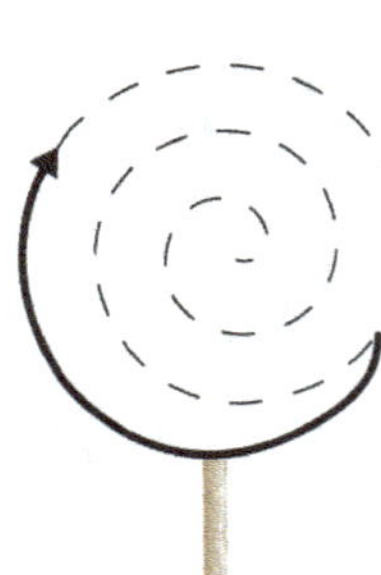

REFLEXION

Why did Massalto's stomach hurt?

IMAGINATION

If there was a large jar what kind of sweets would you put in them? Can you draw it here?

16

Heart & Love

Our heart allows blood to travel across our entire body. Just like a pump… This incredible organ also expresses love. Massalio's friend had once said "My heart is broken." "Can hearts get broken?" Massalio had asked her teacher. Her teacher told her that "Your friend perhaps wanted to tell you that she was upset; it may be good for you to apologize to her and tell her you love her". :)

Can we draw some heart-shapes that represent love and happiness together?

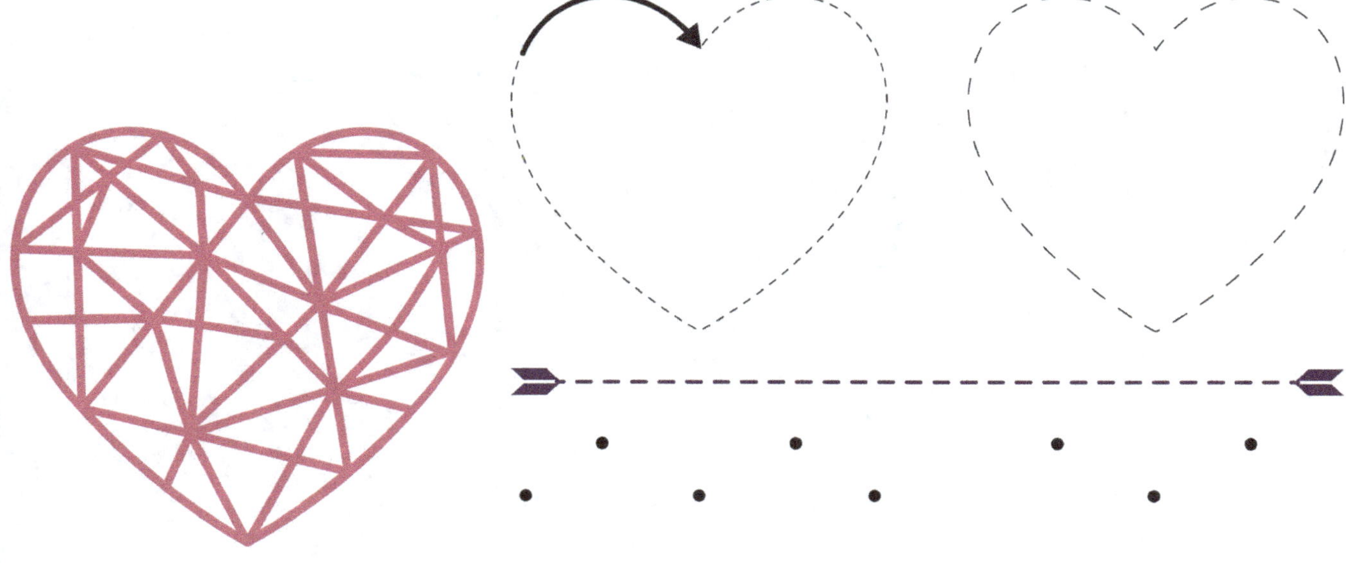

REFLEXION

What does our heart organ do?

IMAGINATION

If you had a jar of love, who or what would you like to put in it? Could you draw it here?

17

Rainbow

Massalio loved rainbows that appeared when the sun and the rain met each other... The rainbow painted such a beautiful red, yellow, blue, orange and green arch across the sky. Massalio wanted to touch the rainbow. Her father then said, "We can try and make our own rainbow." He took the garden hose and started spraying water with his back to the sun. Massalio was running with excitement towards the colors.

Shall we draw a rainbow that has incredible colors together?

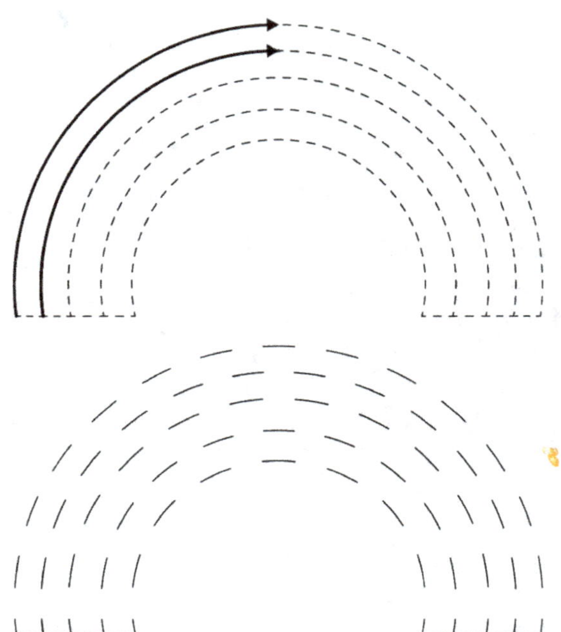

REFLEXION

How is a rainbow formed?

IMAGINATION

If you were to draw a rainbow, what colors would you use? Could you draw it here?

18

Traffic & Cars

Massalio was sitting in the back seat of her mother's car watching the outside... She asked "Why do we have traffic rules?" What do different pavements, roads, signs and lights symbolize? "Rules exist to make life easier and so that we can be more respectful towards one another " replied her mother. Massalio's eyes started following a blue car that was moving past the window.

Are you ready to draw these different roads carefully?

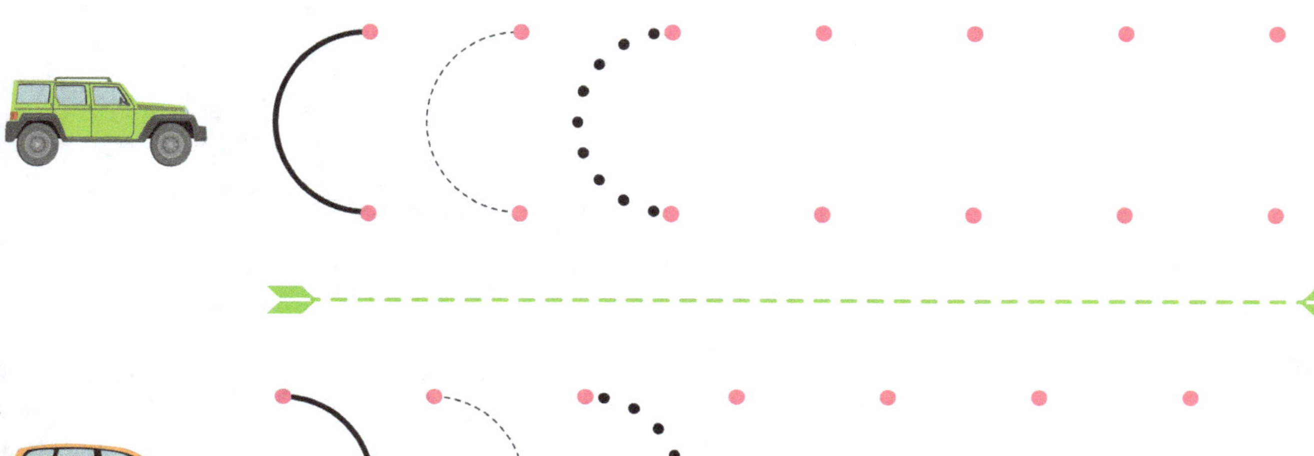

REFLEXION

What colour was the car that Massalio saw?

IMAGINATION

If traffic rules didn't exist, how would cars be on the road? Could you draw it here?

✂ With your scissors, you can cut out and color the medal at the end of the book.

Cows

Cows see objects a little bigger than they appear... They can also hear low frequencies. "How does a cow scratch its back?" wondered Massalto. Her mother said, "Whoever is responsible for taking care of the cows puts a huge brush in a barn and this way, the cows can scratch their backs and heads easily."

What about drawing cows who are jumping up and down and having fun?

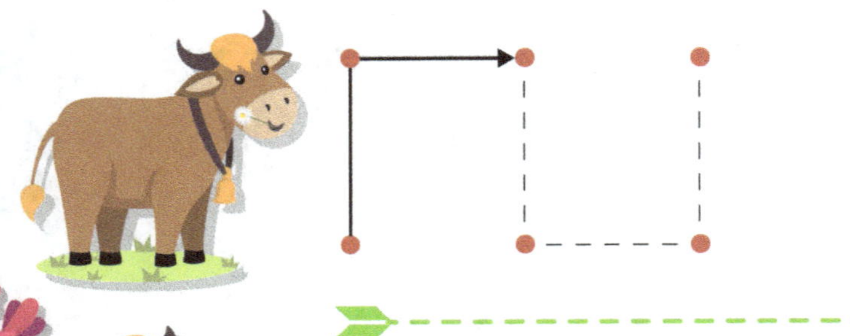

REFLEXION

How do cows see objects?

IMAGINATION

How do cows wander around huge fields? Can you draw it here?

20

✂ With your scissors, you can cut out and color the medal at the end of the book.

Dapkamio was watching a documentary… "Some fish can taste without opening their mouths", the narrator said. Dapkamio was surprised. He knew that the oceans were home to thousands of beings. He imagined that he was a fish. He slowly fell asleep daydreaming that he was swimming amongst the seaweed, playing with the crabs and feeling the waves.

Wouldn't it be amazing if you drew some waves, whilst dreaming about life in the oceans?

REFLEXION

Are fish the only creatures that live in the ocean?

IMAGINATION

What would be the best thing about living under water? Could you draw it here please ?

21

Snow Holiday

Snowflakes are made up of tiny ice crystals… Massalto sat by her window and started watching the falling snow. "Did you know that no single snowflake looks like one another?" asked her father. Massalto was very surprised. She had learnt that each snowflake was completely unique. Just like people. Are you ready to draw the different roads carefully?

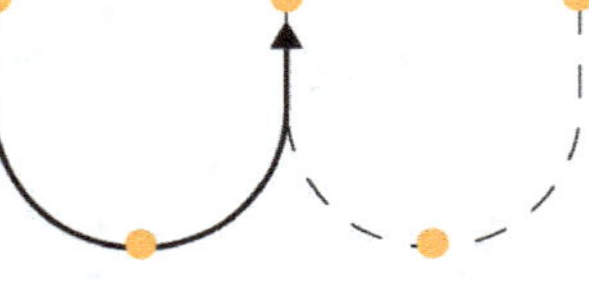

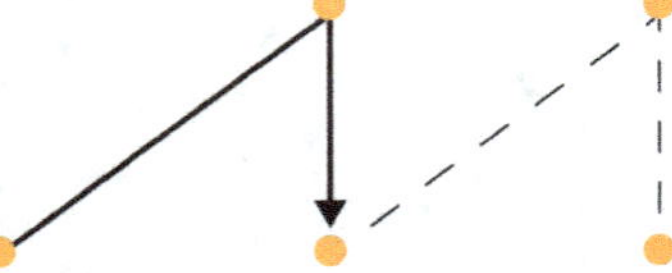

REFLEXION

How are snowflakes formed?

IMAGINATION

If you were a piece of snow clothing, which one would you be? Could you draw it here?

22

The telephone is a device that allows her voice to travel to great distances... The sound is transmitted via radio waves. Did you know that old phones used to be with a cable? Massalio asked "Would we have been able to go everywhere with cable phones? At that very moment, naughty Bubi fell on top of the telephone cables and the cables broke. Massalio laughed out loud and said "I don't think we'll be able to go anywhere now Bubi." :)
Can you please fix the telephone cables that naughty Bubi broke?

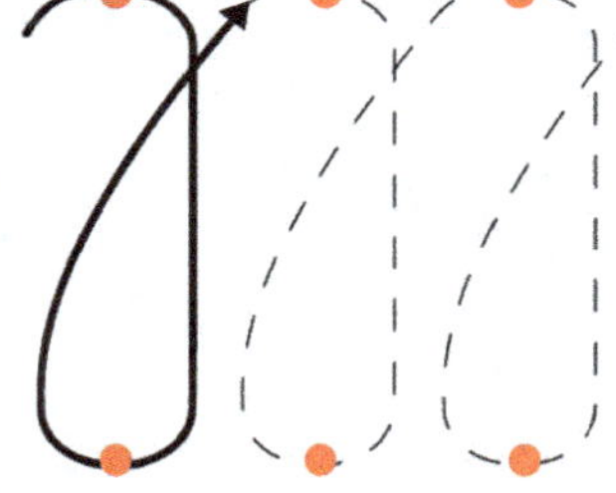

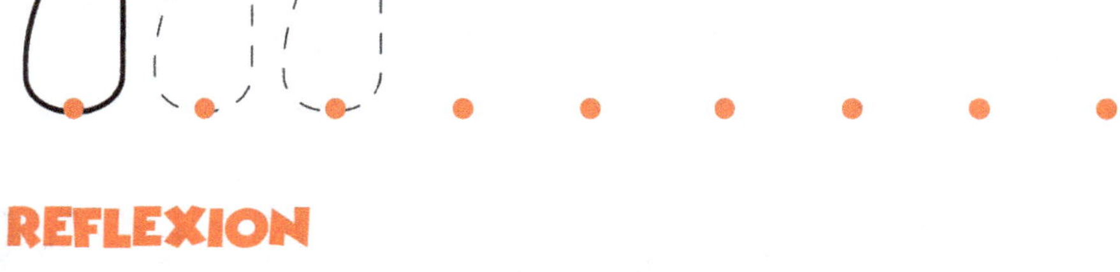

REFLEXION

What do we use our phones for?

IMAGINATION

In the past, what could have been used instead of a phone? Can you draw it here please?

23

Flowers

How are flowers formed? A seed sprouts. A plant is born. This plant grows and a flower bloom. Some flowers don't like the sun. Some, on the other hand, love the sun. "I wonder which flower I should gift my mother?" Dapkamio thought. A red rose? A fragrant daffodil? Or a yellow tulip? He realized the best gift of all is to actually not pick flowers at all, and gifted the drawing he made of flowers to his mother instead. :)

Would you like to draw a colorful and wonderful flower just like Dapkamio?

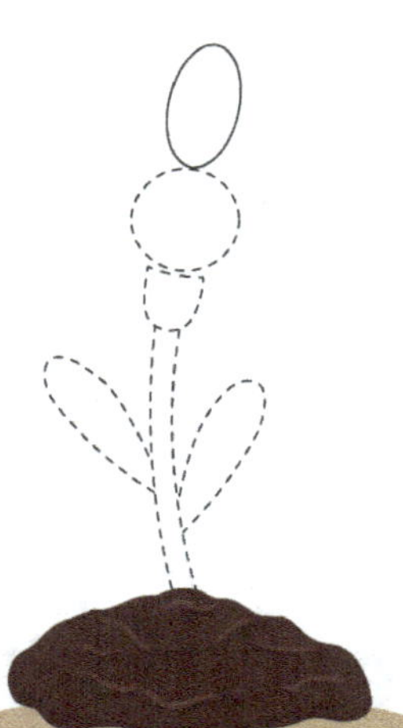

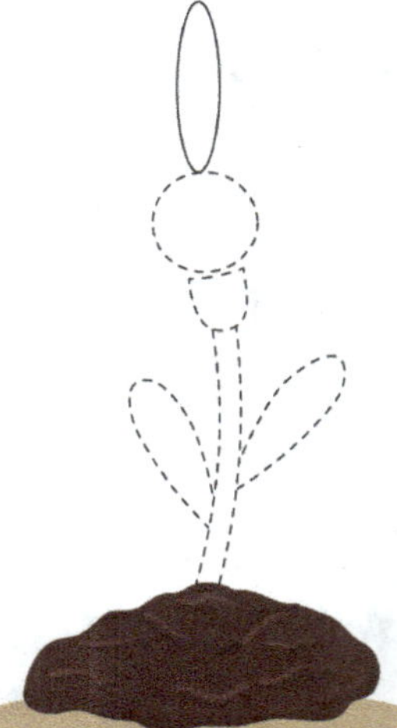

REFLEXION

How are flowers formed?

IMAGINATION

If you had a flower, what would it look like? Can you draw it here?

Seeds can be left in warm water for a certain amount of time. Because of this, the seeds will swell up and their outer shells will soften, making them ready to be germinated. Dapkamio was daydreaming… What would it look like if he had a huge garden? He could grow red apples and fragrant lemons. Dapkamio decided to experiment first in the house garden :)

Can you follow and draw the dots with care and plant the seeds?

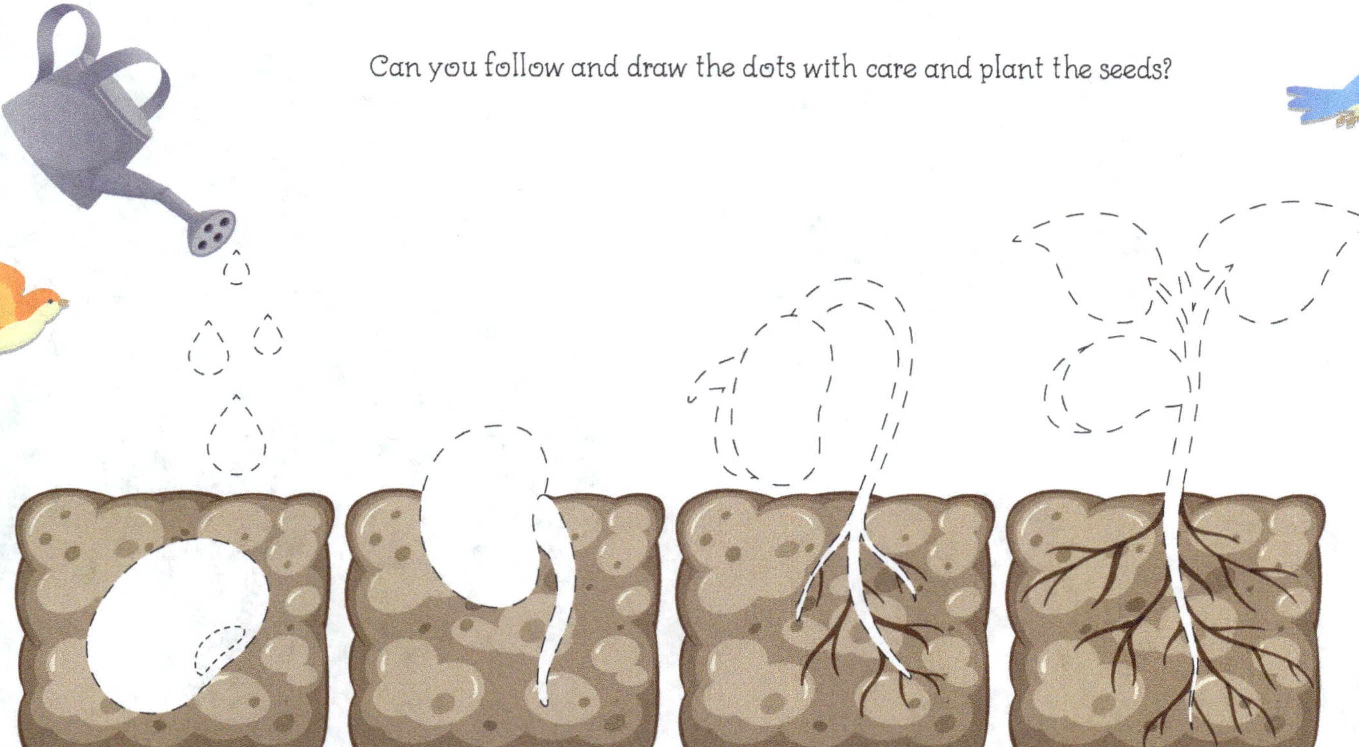

REFLEXION

Why are seeds left in water?

IMAGINATION

If you had a huge garden, what vegetables would you like to plant? Can you draw them here please?

✂ With your scissors, you can cut out and color the medal at the end of the book.

Picnic

That weekend Massalto and Dapkamto decided to go to a picnic. First they needed a picnic basket.

They added some practical foods like fruit and sandwiches. They also brought a ball and a rope.

This way, they would be able to play games. "We are going to have so much fun in the fresh air,"

said Dapkamto… "Come on help me, let's not be late" said Massalto.

What about imagining your own fun picnic and then drawing and painting it?

REFLEXION

What did Massalto and Dapkamto take with them on their picnic?

IMAGINATION

If you were to go to a picnic, what would you take with you? Could you draw it here?

26

Chocolate

A delicious chocolate? That's enough to make Dapkamio happy! To make chocolate, you need to mix and ground cacao dough. Then that is mixed with sugar and milk. It goes through various heating phases which is called tempering. Dapkamio thought about what he should do with the chocolate. Maybe a cake? Maybe eat it with fruit? He was indecisive. :)

Can you help Dapkamio draw a food that he can make with chocolate?

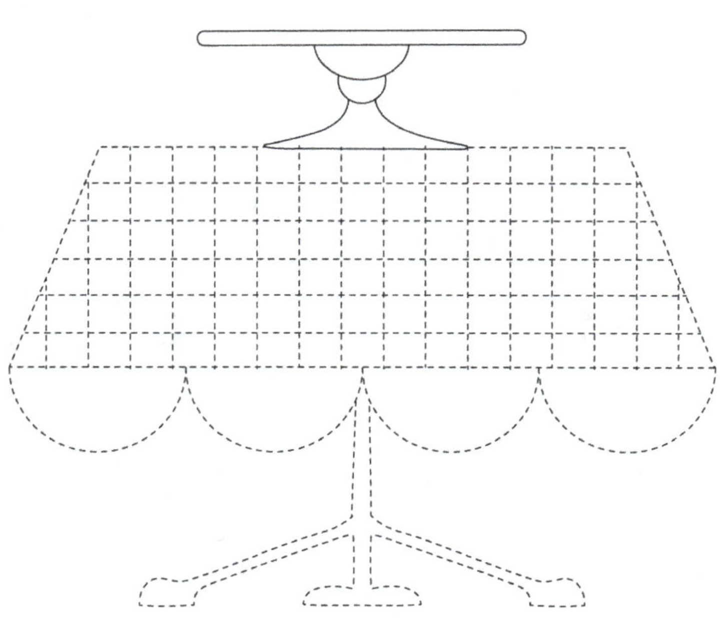

REFLEXION

What do we need to make chocolate?

IMAGINATION

What kind of chocolate would you like to make to make your mother happy?

Can you draw it here please?

✂ With your scissors, you can cut out and color the medal at the end of the book.

Plane

How do planes fly? The shape of the wings of planes creates a difference in the air pressure, and allows the plane to stay in the air. The air that flows around the wings makes it easier for the plane to stay in the air. For this reason, planes must go very quickly. Dapkamio wondered, "If I open my arms and run, could I be as fast as a plane?". He then slowly dozed off whilst daydreaming about this :)

Together, shall we draw what it is we see when we look at the plane window?

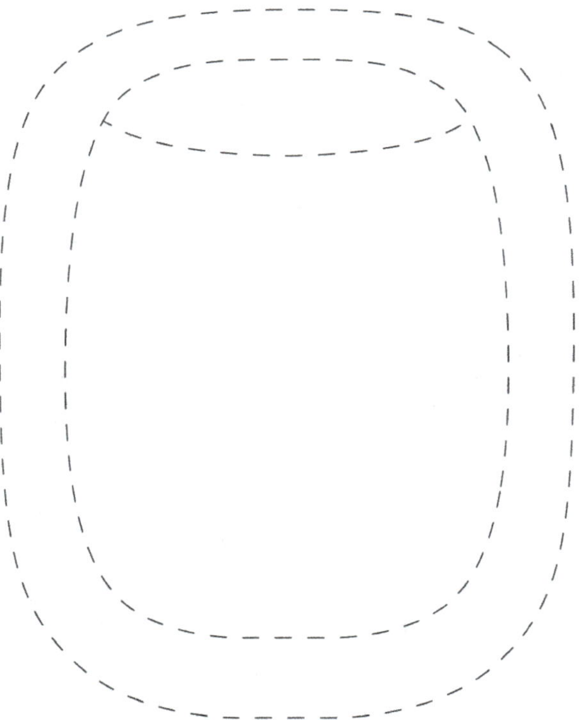

REFLEXION

How do planes fly?

IMAGINATION

Dapkamio was looking outside of the plane window and he was very surprised.

What could he have seen? Can you draw it here?

28

With your scissors, you can cut out and color the medal at the end of the book.

Dreams

We dream as we sleep. Dreams are made up of our moving thoughts just like when we watch cartoons. That night, Dapkamio was sleeping deeply… He was tired from school and needed to rest. What was he seeing in his dream? What was he dreaming of as he sleeps soundly?

Shall we start to draw Dapkamio's colourful dreams?

REFLEXION

When do we dream?

IMAGINATION

What was the most interesting dream you've ever seen up until today?

Could you draw it here please?

29

Robots

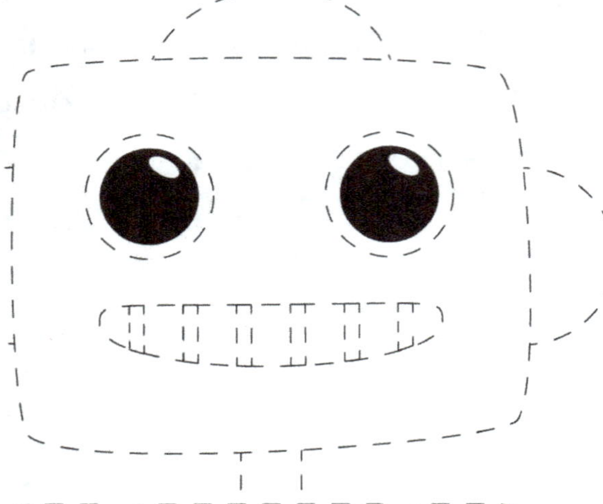

Massalio had watched a film that had robots… He knew that robots were mechanical and electronic devices. He also knew that robots had a computer system within themselves that acted as the brain of the robot. Massalio thought about what she'd do if she had a robot friend. "Instead of searching for my homework on Google, I'd ask my robot friend."

What about drawing and colouring this cute robot that's standing next to you?

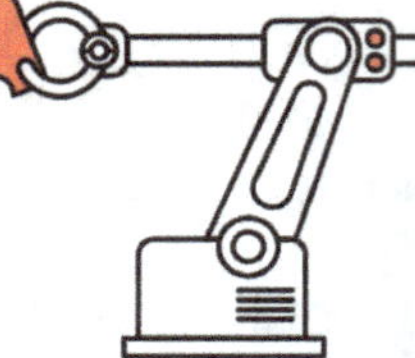

REFLEXION

What is a robot?

IMAGINATION

If you were to design a robot what features would it have? Could you draw it here?

30

Butterflies

The eyes of butterflies are made up of thousands of tiny cells... Because of this, they are very sensitive to colours and flowers. Massalip said "The butterflies' wings are so sweet." She realized that, even if they can't see their own wings, they were beautiful. "We still have beautiful sides to us, even when we can't see ourselves,"

Are you ready to draw and colour unmatched butterfly wings?

REFLEXION

How are butterfly eyes formed?

IMAGINATION

You have wings like a butterfly; but you cannot fly.

What would be the first thing that would come to your mind? Could you draw that here?

31

With your scissors, you can cut out and color the medal at the end of the book.

Glasess

"Is there mist around?" asked Massalto… "I can't see anything", she said. In fact, her glasses had fogged up. She cleaned the lenses of her glasses and put them back on. Now she could see everything a lot clearer. "It would be nice if cats could use glasses because my cat keeps tripping on stones in front of them," said Massalto.

Who owns these glasses? Could you draw the person you are imagining?

REFLEXION

Why can't Massalto see around?

IMAGINATION

If you were to design glasses for animals, what would it look like? Could you draw it here?

✂ With your scissors, you can cut out and color the medal at the end of the book.

Hair

Massalio looked at the people walking by on the street… Everyone had different hairstyles. Our hair protects our skin against weather conditions such as rain and wind. It also allows us to express ourselves. Some people have curly hair. Some people like long hair; some like short hair. The most important thing is to be able to love one another with our differences.

What colours are you going to use to draw this cute child's hair?

REFLEXION

Why do we have hair?

IMAGINATION

If we didn't use a brush, what would our hair look like? Could you draw it here?

33

Massalio had learnt about sand in her geography lesson… Sand was tiny rock pieces. These pieces are carried to the rivers with rain, and as they are carried towards the sea, they turn into sand. They then pile up on beaches with the movement of the winds. Massalio wanted to make a sand castle. However, she was going to have to move a little further away from the sea shore. She didn't want the waves to destroy her sand castle. :)

How about drawing a sand castle and bucket to say hello to the holidays?

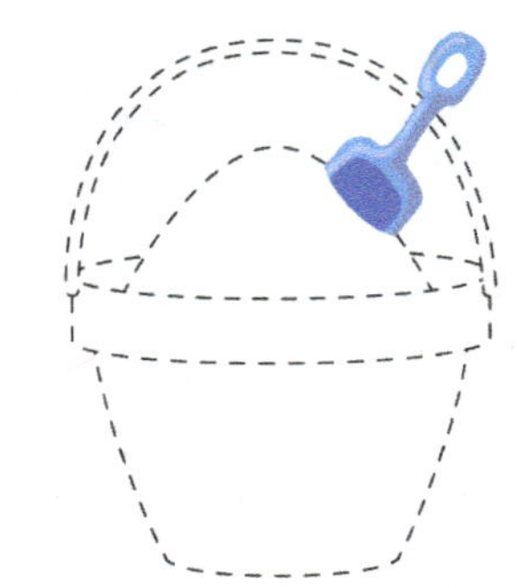
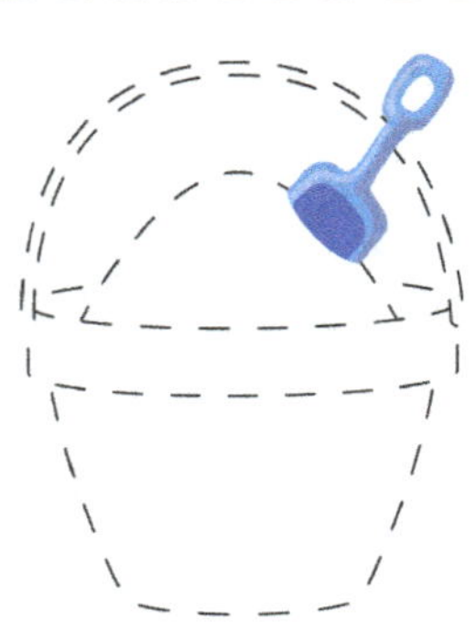

REFLEXION

Why did Massalio move a little away from the sea shore?

IMAGINATION

If you were to draw a sand castle in which people lived, what would that look like?
Could you draw that here?

The oceans are the habitat of thousands of fish. "We need to keep our environment clean," said Massalip. "We shouldn't throw our plastic bottles and other rubbish into the sea," she added. "The rubbish we throw could get stuck in the throats of fish and could harm them" she said and then picked up some rubbish on the beach and put it in a plastic bag. :)

Show us how you would get rid of marine pollution through finishing this drawing.

REFLEXION

What did Massalto do to keep the environment clean?

IMAGINATION

If you had a wish, what kind of sea would you like to live in? Can you explain through a drawing?

✂ With your scissors, you can cut out and color the medal at the end of the book.

Fruits

Fruits are usually eaten raw… They are colorful and delicious. Since they are a high source of vitamins, we eat fruit often. Massalio thought "If all fruits were the same color how would we differentiate them?" She realized that she would be able to tell them apart through their taste. "A watermelon is very watery and sweet, whereas a greengage plum is sour" she said as she smiled.

Are you ready to pair the same fruit together?

REFLEXION

Why do we eat fruits?

IMAGINATION

What type of fruit would surprise you if you saw it? Draw it here.

Animal Feed

Dapkamio fell into deep thoughts… Why do all animals eat different foods? Rabbits have very firm front teeth. They love crunchy foods. Dogs love to run. They run after bones that are thrown far away. Dapkamio said "I love all types of food but not all animals may like to eat burritos like me" said Dapkamio.

What food matches which animal? Can you help them by drawing?

REFLEXION

What type of foods do rabbits like?

IMAGINATION

If dogs could fly how would it be? Could you show us through drawing?

✂ With your scissors, you can cut out and color the medal at the end of the book.

Camp

Massalto had gone camping with her family... The weather was gorgeous and the stars were brightening up the night sky. Massalto watched on carefully as her father lit a fire. Her mother said "You should be careful with some plants, they could be poisonous." Massalto was excited for the night. She was going to daydream and fall asleep listening to the forest sounds.

How about drawing different camp objects and colouring them in?

REFLEXION

Where did Massalto go with her family?

IMAGINATION

If night was constant, what would life look like? Could you explain through drawing?

38

Massalio realised someone was following her as she was playing ball… She ran quickly. She was out of breath. As she said "Hey who are you?" and stopped, she realised it was her shadow. Her shadow that had formed in the space where the sun's rays weren't touching, made her laugh. "Since fish are in the sea, they probably don't have shadows" she thought. :)

Can you match different sports objects with their shadows?

REFLEXION

What was Massalio afraid of?

IMAGINATION

If you were a shadow, what kind of shadow would you like to be? Can you tell us through drawing?

Massalio found out that ducklings were different from their mothers… All ducks feathers were waterproof. But the ducklings were yellow, and their mother was white. Massalio's mother said "Sometimes we look like one another, sometimes we don't look like one another."

Massalio joyously watched the ducklings swimming with their mother.

Can you help the mother duck reach her ducklings the best way?

REFLEXION

What colour is the mother duck?

IMAGINATION

If you were in the duck's position and your cap fell into the lake, how would you save it? Could you tell us through drawing?

Apple

The fruits that insects eat are healthier... Because living beings gravitate towards healthy food. However, this interest from the insects led to the fruits going off. Dapkamio thought. If he was a caterpillar what fruit would he like to eat? "I'd dive straight into an apple, because apple's are delicious," he said. However, he didn't know how he would find the way out of the fruit once he had gotten inside. :)
Can you help the hungry caterpillar find its way to eat the apple?

REFLEXION

What fruit would Dapkamio like to eat?

IMAGINATION

If you were a caterpillar, what kind of apple would you like to eat?
Could you explain through drawing?

# Numbers

Twin siblings 1 and 0 were playing hide-and-seek in the forest...
1 tagged her sister. Her sister asked "I had hidden behind the tree,
butyou found me. So, what season do you think is when trees
produceleaves?" Her sister said, "Nature awakens in spring, the sun
heatseverywhere up, I'll tag you during that season as well."
The twins had a lot of fun. :)
Wouldn't it be great if we can draw the number 0 before hiding
behind the tree?

REFLEXION

What season do trees turn green?

IMAGINATION

If you were invisible, what would you like to do? Could you draw it here please?

42

1 and 0, two sweet siblings… 1 said to his brother 0, "How does the Earth go around the Sun?" Then 0 said, "It takes the Earth 1 year around to go around the Sun. Just like how you turn when you turn 1 years old." Both siblings looked at the sky and smiled. :) What about writing 1 by the Earth going around the sun.

REFLEXION

How does the Earth go around the Sun?

IMAGINATION

How would you explain what the sun is to those people living in cold countries? Could you draw it here?

43

Smart siblings 1 and 2 were in the car… They looked at the car infront when their mother stopped at the red light. "Mother, whydid you stop?" said 1… "Because when the red light comes on, cars must stop to make way for pedestrians" replied their mother. "True! Then there won't be a mix-up in the traffic" said 2….The green light came on and they continued on their way. :) Shall we write 2 as we imagine the cars in the front of the traffic jam?

REFLEXION

When do cars stop on the road?

IMAGINATION

If animals could drive, what animal do you think would be the best at driving?

44

Two good friends 1 and 3 went on an aquarium trip together...
There were plenty of fish and water creatures there. 1 excitedly said
"Did you know that fish breathe through their gills?" 3 said "I would
love to be able to open my eyes inside the water just like a fish."
They had a very nice day together. :)
Shall we write 3 to say hi to the fish swimming
contentedly in the sea?

REFLEXION

How do fish breathe?

IMAGINATION

If you were to design a toy for fish, what features would it have? Could you draw it here?

45

1 and 4 are very close friends… They went to the library that day together. The books had been placed side-by-side. "Why must we read?" asked 1… "Because books tell us about the world. We learn about important information from books" replied 4… "But this isn't enough," he added. "We need to be able to practice those good things we have learnt in life," he said. 1 jumped from his place and said "I'm also going to write a book." :)
Shall we draw a perfect 4, just how perfect these books look side-by-side.

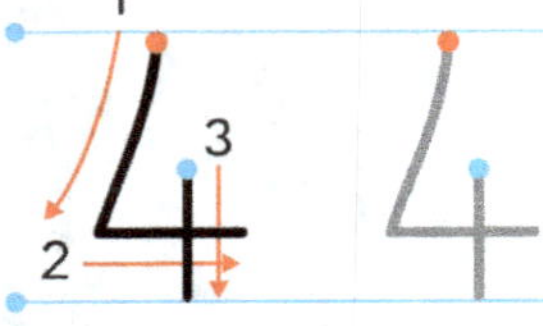

REFLEXION

Why should we read books?

IMAGINATION

How do you think people learned when there were no books? Could you draw it here?

46

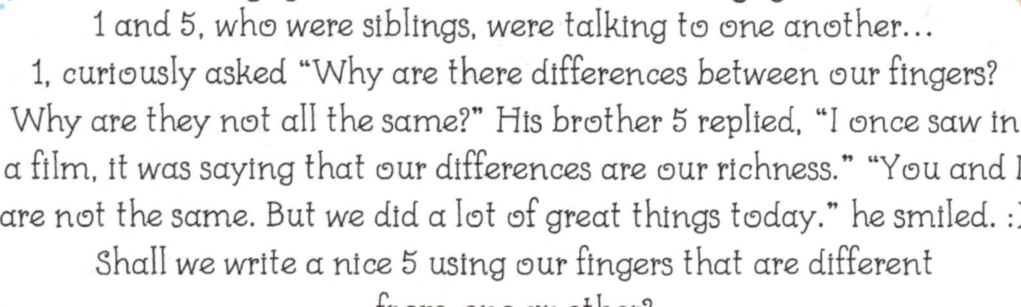

REFLEXION

Why do we have differences between our fingers?

IMAGINATION

If you had to design a glove to keep your hands cool during warm weather, what would you add onto the glove? Could you draw it here?

47

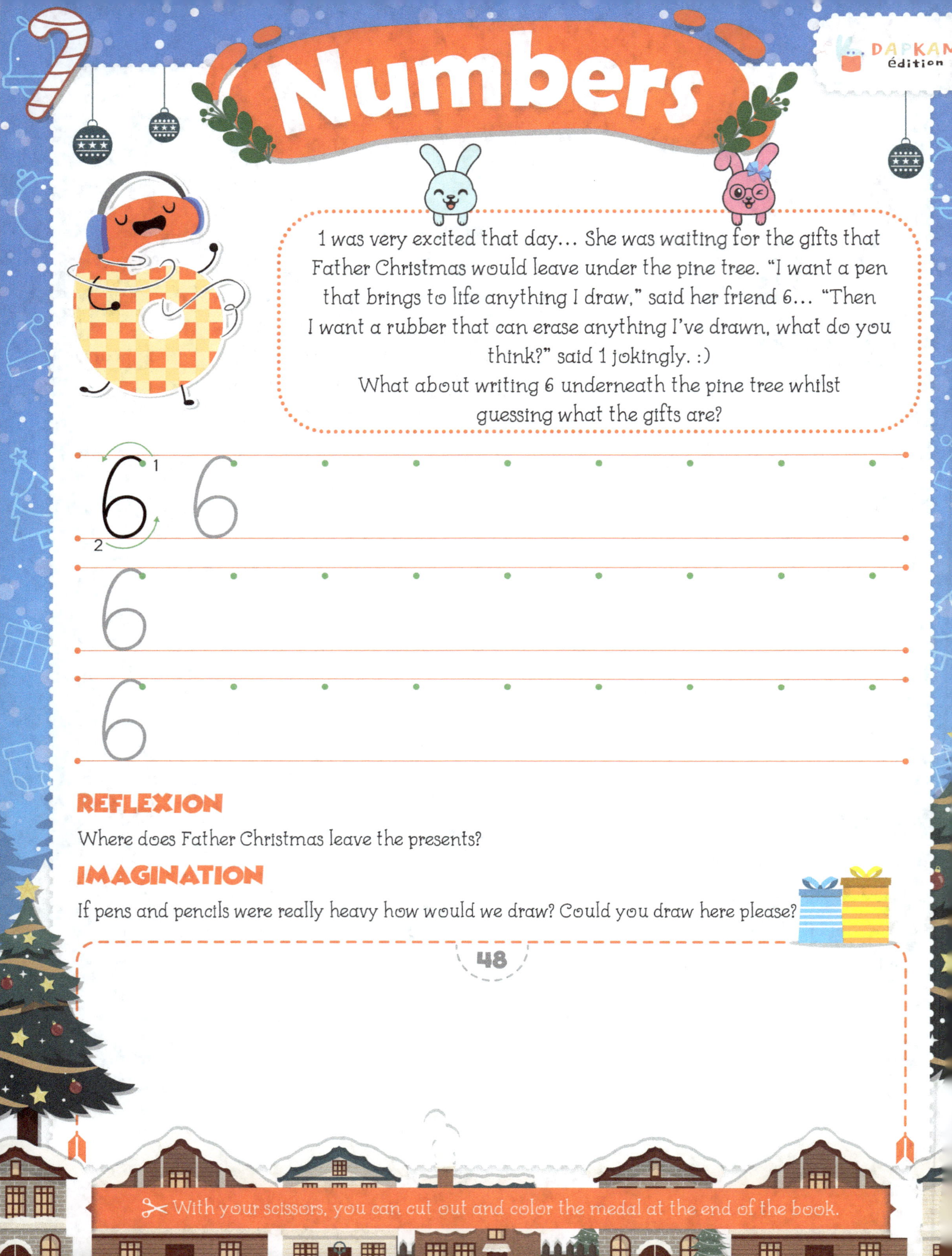

Numbers

1 was very excited that day... She was waiting for the gifts that Father Christmas would leave under the pine tree. "I want a pen that brings to life anything I draw," said her friend 6... "Then I want a rubber that can erase anything I've drawn, what do you think?" said 1 jokingly. :)
What about writing 6 underneath the pine tree whilst guessing what the gifts are?

REFLEXION

Where does Father Christmas leave the presents?

IMAGINATION

If pens and pencils were really heavy how would we draw? Could you draw here please?

48

Numbers

1 and 7 were walking towards the bakery that morning…
The confectioner was baking cakes and bread after combining
ingredients with one another. 1 looked over with an appetite and
asked "If you were a confectioner, what kind of cake would you
make?" 7 then replied "I'd make it in the shape of a toy, no one
would understand it was a toy until I cut it with a knife." :)
What about drawing a nice 7 after imagining the cakes?

REFLEXION

How are cakes made?

IMAGINATION

You are a baker, what kind of cakes would you make for children? Could you draw them here?

49

1 and 8 went biking together… A cat had fallen from a tree and had been injured. They thought about calling 18 to ask help from the fire department. Panicked, 1 said, "We can call 112 to get fire and health help in Europe". Aid teams arrived quickly and started treating the cat immediately. 1 and 8 were grateful to have helped. :) The cat that fell from the top of the tree is better now; shall we write 8 for them?

REFLEXION

What number must we call when we need help?

IMAGINATION

How do children who do not know the same language play together? Can you draw it here?

✂ With your scissors, you can cut out and color the medal at the end of the book.

1 and 9 were playing in the garden before breakfast... A puppy came up to them and sniffed them. Dogs have a very strong sense of smell. Their olfactory memory is really good. "Maybe he may remember us years later" laughed 1... "Maybe he also knows his own mother by her smell" thought 9. :)
How about writing a nice 9 together before going to breakfast?

REFLEXION

Why can't dogs forget the people they see?

IMAGINATION

If you had a strong sense of smell, what would you like to smell? Could you draw it here please?

51

Dapkamio
1
Dapkamio
2
Dapkamio
3
Dapkamio
4
Dapkamio
5
Dapkamio
6

Congratulations
Congratulations
Congratulations
Congratulations
Congratulations
Congratulations

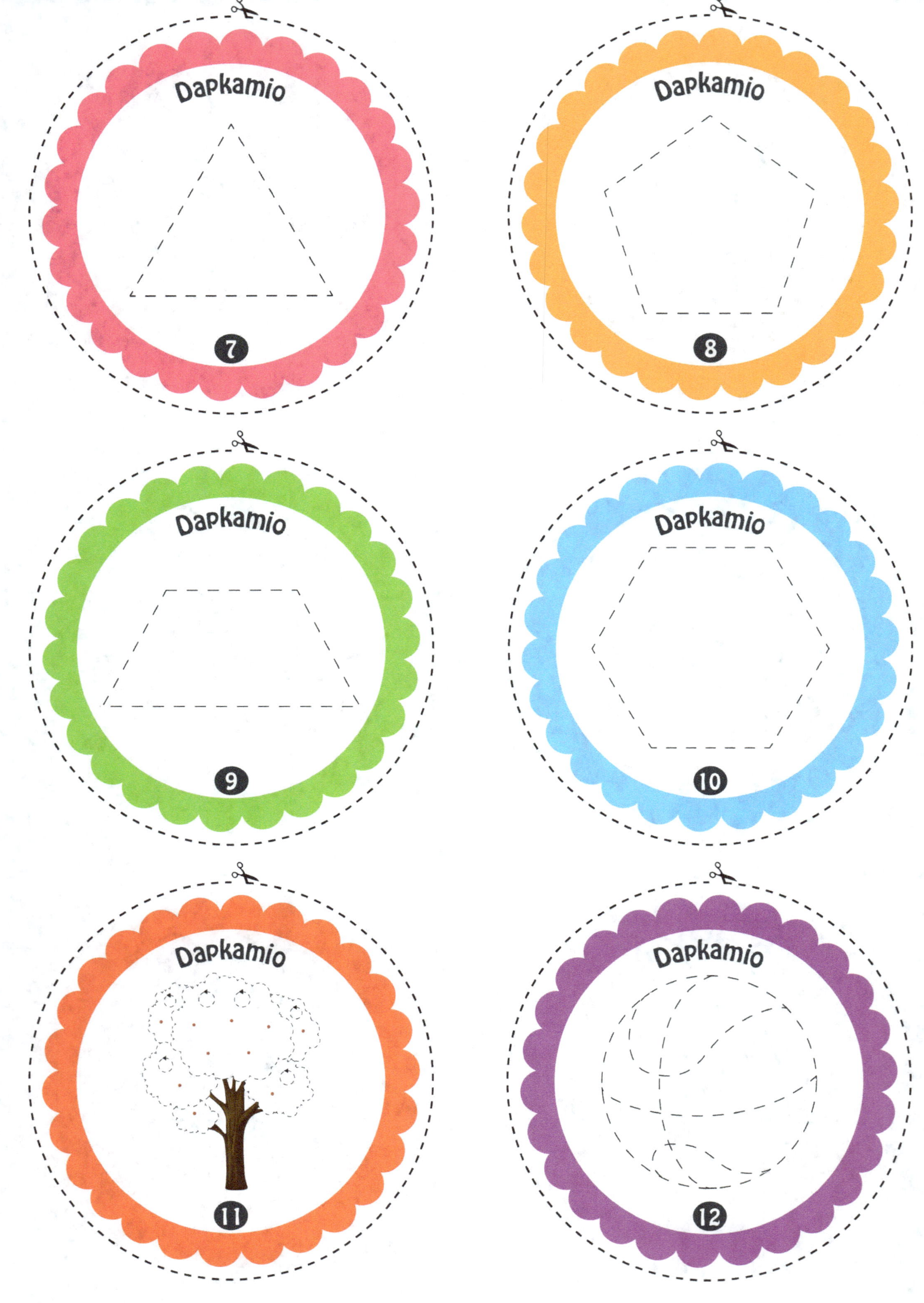

Dapkamio
Dapkamio
Dapkamio
Dapkamio
Dapkamio
Dapkamio
7
8
9
10
11
12

Congratulations
Congratulations
Congratulations
Congratulations
Congratulations
Congratulations

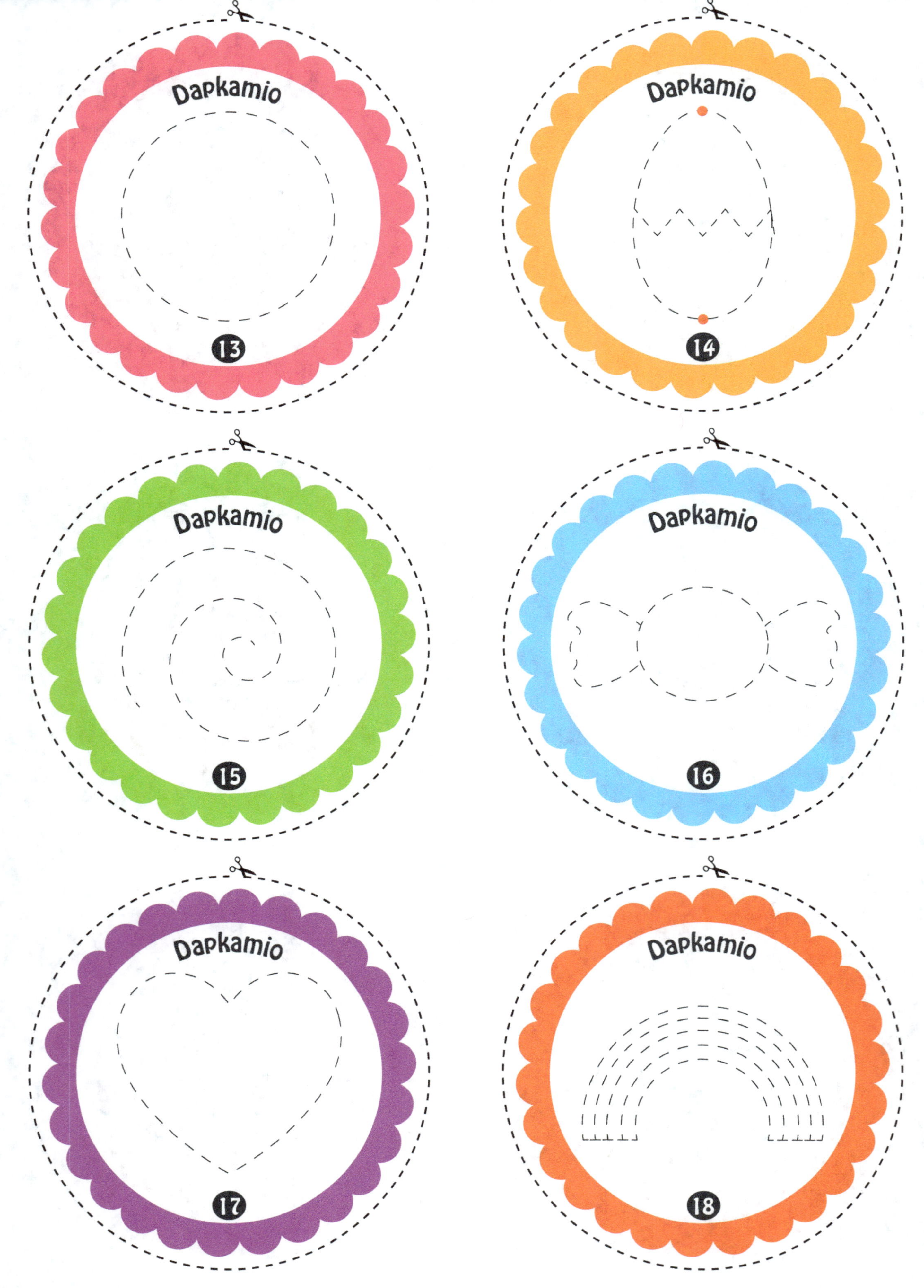

Dapkamio
13
Dapkamio
14
Dapkamio
15
Dapkamio
16
Dapkamio
17
Dapkamio
18

Congratulations
Congratulations
Congratulations
Congratulations
Congratulations
Congratulations

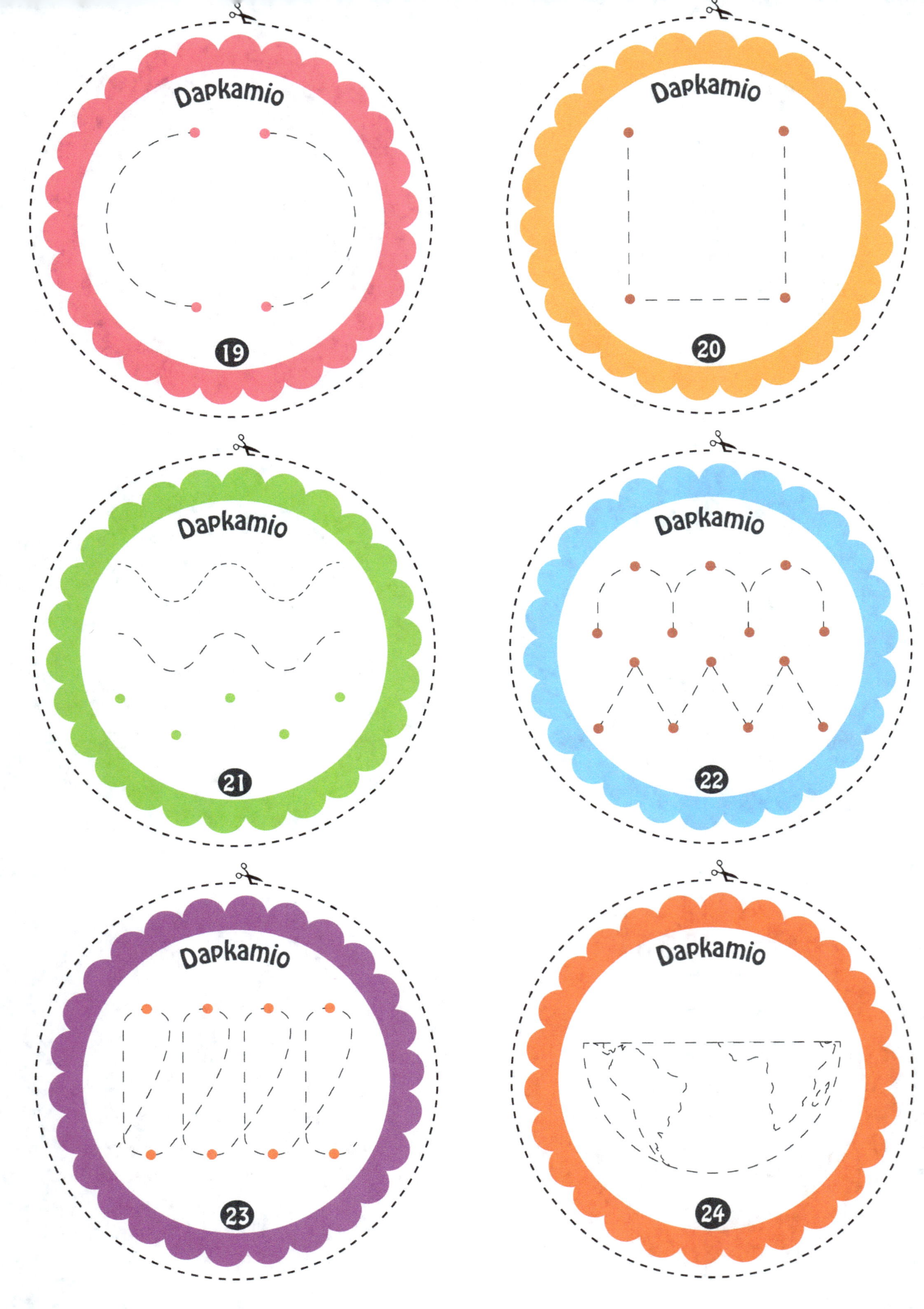

Dapkamio
19
Dapkamio
20
Dapkamio
21
Dapkamio
22
Dapkamio
23
Dapkamio
24

Congratulations
Congratulations
Congratulations
Congratulations
Congratulations
Congratulations

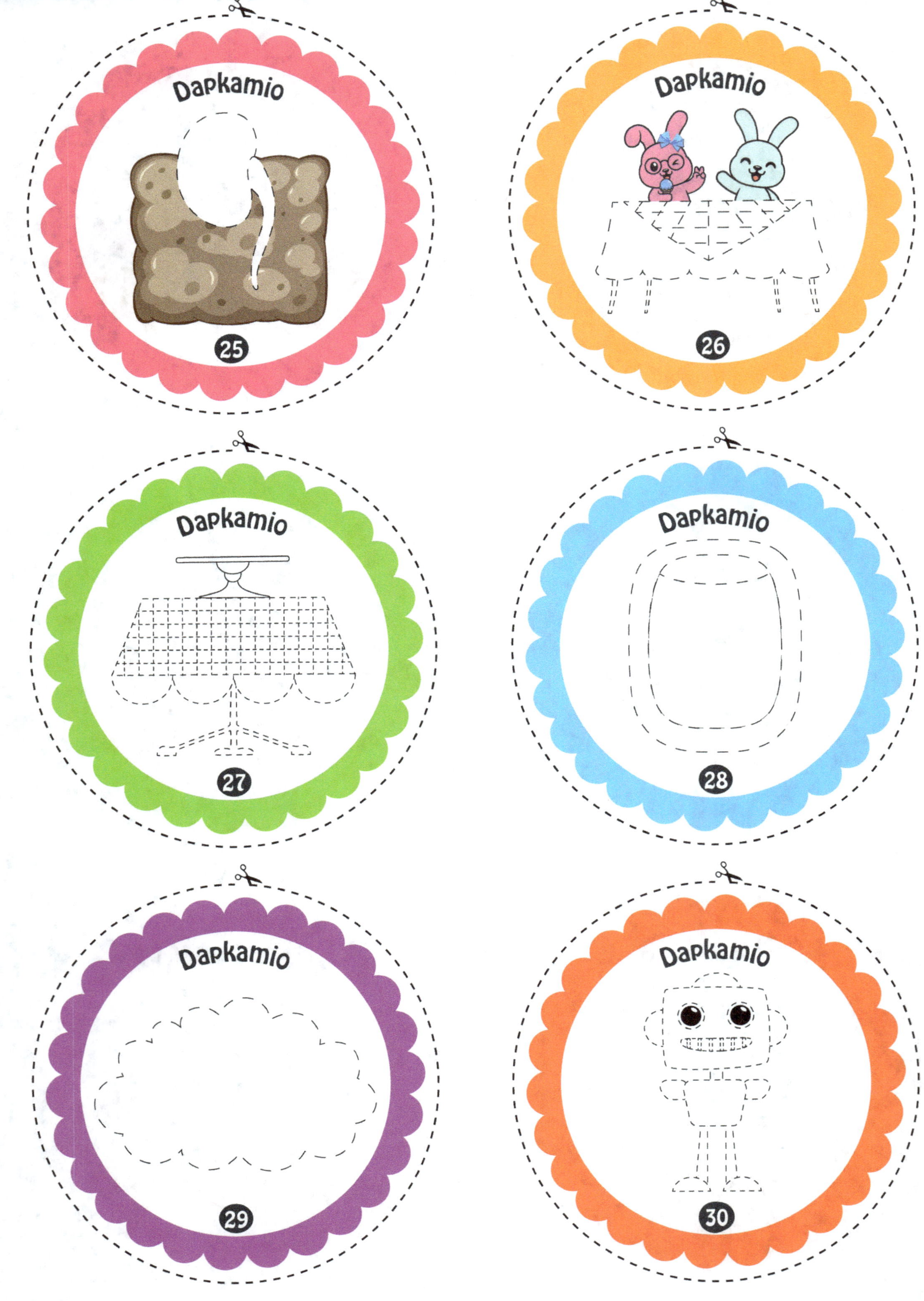
Dapkamio
25
Dapkamio
26
Dapkamio
27
Dapkamio
28
Dapkamio
29
Dapkamio
30

Congratulations
Congratulations
Congratulations
Congratulations
Congratulations
Congratulations

Dapkamio
Dapkamio
31
32
Dapkamio
Dapkamio
33
34
Dapkamio
Dapkamio
35
36

Congratulations
Congratulations
Congratulations
Congratulations
Congratulations
Congratulations

Dapkamio
37
Dapkamio
38
Dapkamio
39
Dapkamio
40
Dapkamio
41
Dapkamio
42

Congratulations
Congratulations
Congratulations
Congratulations
Congratulations
Congratulations

Dapkamio
1
43
Dapkamio
2
44
Dapkamio
3
45
Dapkamio
4
46
Dapkamio
5
47
Dapkamio
6
48

Congratulations
Congratulations
Congratulations
Congratulations
Congratulations
Congratulations

Dapkamio
7
49

Dapkamio
8
50

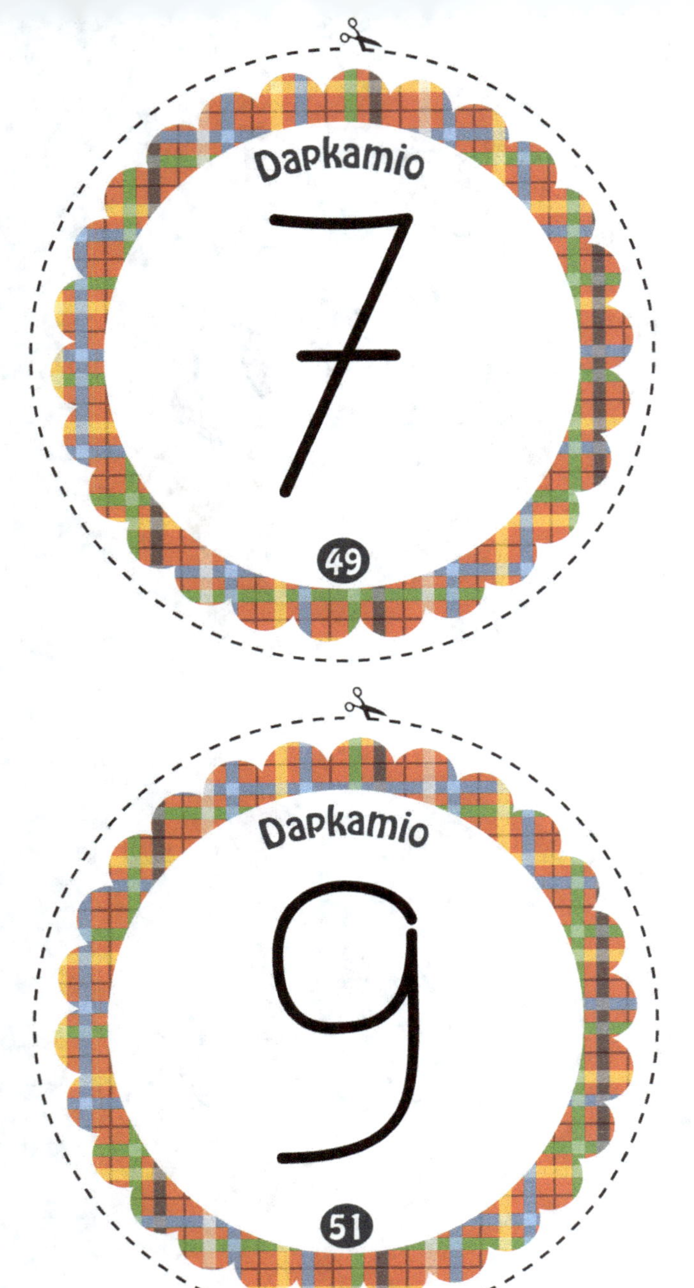

Dapkamio
9
51

Congratulations

Congratulations
Congratulations